Let's Go Shopping!

Contents

Let's Go Shopping!	2
Bartering	4
Money	6
Bargaining	7
Shopping Centres	8
Markets and Bazaars	10
Floating Markets	14
Internet Shopping	16
The Old Bridge	18
Shopping in Antarctica	20
Shopping Around the World	22
Glossary and Index	24

THOMSON

NELSON

Australia · Canada · Mexico · Singapore · Spain · United Kingdom · United States

Let's Go Shopping!

All around the world, people go shopping!
Many kinds of **goods** are bought and sold,
every day.

People buy food to eat and clothes to wear.
They also buy goods for their homes and
presents for their families and friends.

THE NORTHERN ...

824 0491

Shopping at a market.

All around the world, goods are bought and sold in lots of different ways!

Shopping on the Internet.

Bartering

Sometimes people swap goods instead of using **money** to buy them. This is called **bartering**. People bartered long before money was invented. Bartering has been around for thousands of years.

Long ago, Roman soldiers were often paid in salt for their work, instead of money.

Today, in places where people do not have much money, bartering helps them get things they need.

5

Money

Money was invented over 4000 years ago! Metals, such as gold and silver, were used to make coins.

Then, in China, about 1000 years ago, paper money was invented.

Today, people from around the world use different types of money.

Ancient coins.

Bargaining

Before we buy something, we usually know how much it will cost. But in some parts of the world, people **bargain** with each other over the cost of goods.

Traders ask a high price for their goods. Shoppers offer to pay much less. Then the traders and shoppers bargain with each other until everyone is happy with the price.

Shopping

Some indoor shopping centres have cinemas, play areas and places to eat. Indoor shopping centres are found in most countries.

Centres

Have you ever visited an indoor shopping centre? Indoor shopping centres are found in big cities and towns where many people live. There are many different kinds of shops inside them.

People can buy all their goods at an indoor shopping centre without going outside. It does not matter if the weather is hot or cold.

Markets and...

A market in China.

For thousands of years, people have shopped at **markets** and **bazaars**.

Markets are found in most countries. Traders bring their goods to the markets. They sell them from small shops or **stalls**.

Markets are set up in streets or open places. It is easy for people who live nearby to come and shop.

Many goods sold at markets are home-made or home-grown.

...Bazaars

Some parts of the world are famous for their large bazaars. Turkey has many bazaars. Tourists come from other countries just to visit them.

Hundreds of traders stand beside their shops, offering to sell their goods to people who pass by. They sell beautiful things, such as jewellery and **Turkish carpets**.

Traders in Turkey give shoppers a cup of tea when they come to buy their goods!

In some countries, markets are held on water.

Thailand has many rivers and canals. Traders who live by the water bring their goods to market in a boat. These markets are called floating markets.

At floating markets, traders sit in their boats along the edges of canals or rivers. Shoppers come to buy fresh food, such as tropical fruits.

Floating Markets

Delicious noodles and hot coffee are also sold from boats at floating markets. Many people enjoy sitting at the water's edge, eating the food and drinks that they buy.

Internet

Today, we can use a computer to shop on the Internet!

We can visit different websites and choose what we want to buy. Small pictures show us what the goods look like. We can order them and have them delivered to our homes or even sent to a friend.

When shopping on the Internet, we pay for our goods with a **credit card**.

Shopping

This bridge is in Italy. It is called the **Ponte Vecchio,** which means 'old bridge'.

Hundreds of years ago, traders set up small shops on the bridge. It was a good place to own a shop. People who crossed the bridge often stopped to buy things.

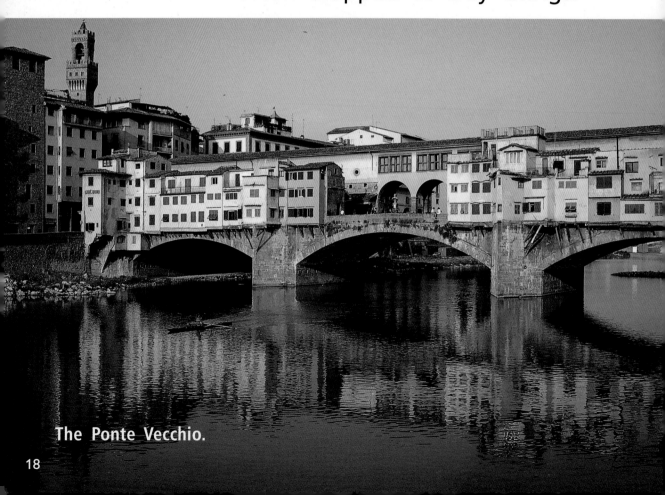

The Ponte Vecchio.

Bridge

Today, traders still have small shops on the old bridge. They sell jewellery and other beautiful things.

Jewellery inside a shop on the Ponte Vecchio.

Shopping in Antarctica

A base camp in Antarctica

In some parts of the world, there are no shops! People living and working in Antarctica use the Internet to order their goods from other countries.

In winter, the sea around Antarctica is frozen. Ships cannot bring goods to the people who are there. They must wait until the weather is warmer for their goods to arrive.

It takes many months for goods to arrive in Antarctica.

Goods being unloaded from a ship in Antarctica.

GREEN WAVE

Shopping Around the World

United States
of America

There are many different
ways and places to shop,
all around the world!
Which is your favourite?

Index

Antarctica 20–21
bargaining 7
bartering 4–5
bazaars 11,
    12–13
floating markets
    14–15
Internet
    shopping 16, 20
Italy 18–19
markets 11,
    12–13, 14–15
money 4, 5, 6
Ponte Vecchio
    18–19
shopping centres
    8–9
Thailand 14–15
traders 11, 12–13,
    14–15, 18–19
Turkey 12–13

Glossary

bargain to agree with someone on a price for something that is for sale

bartering swapping goods with someone, rather than using money

bazaars special markets found in some countries

credit card a special card from the bank used instead of money

goods things that people buy

markets places, usually outdoors, where people buy and sell goods

money something that is used to buy goods

Ponte Vecchio [say *pont-air vet-key-oh*] a very old bridge in Italy

stalls very small shops, often at markets

Turkish carpets special carpets, made in Turkey, that have beautiful patterns